D1662067

FABRICATING SHADOWS

Fabricating Shadows

MARC SQUIRES

Library of Congress Control Number:		2017919360
ISBN:	Hardcover	978-1-5434-7260-8
	Softcover	978-1-5434-7261-5
	eBook	978-1-5434-7262-2

Print information available on the last page.

Rev. date: 03/07/2018

To order additional copies of this book, contact:
Xlibris
1-888-795-4274
www.Xlibris.com
Orders@Xlibris.com
772014

Contents

Just Imagine

The hardest part
Is knowing what to say
In the depths of solitude
This place I create

Imagination running free
As these thoughts turn to words
Anything could happen
When this mind's at work

Carefully analyzing
Looking around
Surrounded by madness
I cringe then smile

This place I love so free
As devious as my dementia
Deception is the key

To exist in this world
You can't take
Nothing for granted
Sell your soul cheap
At the price of their semantics

Plots thicken with every breath
You can absorb it so kindly
To let go of regret

This world that you knew
Crumbles before your eyes
A wasteland of pity
Reflecting the guilt you hide

It's a story you know all too well
To bare or not
It's what you love

Fueling fear
Eyes gleaming with pain
Constantly testing the theory
Only agony awaits

Self-induced
Some might think it's strange
In life
We all suffer
We pick and you choose are ways

How It Began

I can't fight it anymore
Emotions that build
Never settle
Seeping out my pores

Trying to just plea
Fighting this manic that runs deep
Escape isn't the plan
It's like I've been gone for so long
Within my head I call home
Most wouldn't understand

Through my reflection I'm seeing
It's like glancing at the demon
Thinking this cage would keep me safe
Within the depth of these eyes
Rests a key he holds tight
Unlocking that door
Now my fears are just free

Why fight what I feel
When I embrace all that's not real
It swallows who I am
My reflection conceals
The truth my heart shields
Only in deep thought I understand
I question what my soul needs

Restless Nights

Every dream slips away
Up and down for no reason
My soul screams in pain

Dawn's approaching
Shiver through my thoughts
This mind keeps racing
The voices won't stop

Captivating
Eyes open wide
Where's my sense of control
This conscience noosed tight

Fears displayed scene by scene
This repetitive scenario
Falling out of reach

Thought of no sequence
Randomly embraced
Deception always taunting
Searching to escape

All this fury that lurks within
Hopelessly infused
Maybe there's a way to bleed sins
Or free will to choose

So strung with the term it's in vain
Building my resilience
Yet the pain won't fade

All I ever asked for
Was to simply close my eyes
Dream here in peace
Instead
My soul dies

Black Again

What's the difference
Casting myself away
Or staying here to suffer
Till the end of my days
Searching astray
Looking for something to ease
For all I create
So little to redeem
My world turns black again

So much relates
So much retains
All these feelings I run from
Before I crumble in vain
Time wasted
As moments slip away
Everything's unstable
Alone I break

If I could view myself
For what others feel are true
Live by their inspiration
Walking so proud to prove

Injecting their blood
Through these veins
To live by their strength
To know I can change

Finding purpose
Within those moments of fear
The little hope that I carry
Dissolves my tears

It's so cold

Turning black again
So much I can't take
When it all pertains
To every feeling I've lived through
I can't crumble in vain

Strength falters through despair
Situations leave me
Physically impaired

It's all gone black again
All the time I waste
Moments slip away
Everything's unstable
I can't fade into the shadows in vain

Addicted

What's up with my life again?
This new meaning of betrayal
My reflection
I thought was a friend
Through your eyes
I repent
Some things can't be ignored
When I face you days on end
It haunts me to the core

Sheltered life
The perfect cover
Always wrapped up in some mess
Fooled by my own endeavors

To ignore what's at stake
Reaching to satisfy
Like a fiend in dismay
You'll never obey
As you're caught between two worlds
Escaping your past
Through every hit that won't last
Don't look at me
like I'm the fool

I'm just the vessel
Whom you choose to abuse
Spotted in plain view
The world can see the truth

Awake to a new day
I turn toward you my friend
Help me get passed
The shacking
The sweating
Won't end

Everything you hide from
Patiently awaits
Every thought that you buried
resurfaced to escape

I see you my friend
My reflection I hold so dear
Just get through this phase
As you awake here each day
Your soul need not fear

Through the Eyes of Me

Intrigued by all that's unique
Pictures of so many faces
That we'll never come to greet

A smile is all we hold
To believe we're masked with innocents
The truth is we'll never show

We find comfort in all who hears
Pushing thoughts
Into those who care

We claim we're all just saints
Inside
We're demons
Waiting to be uncaged

So place your thoughts upon this world
Tell your secrets
There's so much they wish to know

Lend your voice into my ear
Like a whisper into the darkness
Free what you fear

Cast away into your fate
To think that I listen
It's your own mistake

Here
I feel no control
Like a temptress suited
To find my pawns

Deliver yourself into my flame
Fueled by our intentions
That are never tame

My only wish is to have you
Just free yourself

Upon the Path

I'm walking upon the path of darkness
All I sense are lost dreams
Betrayed by my conscience
Falling for false leads
Reality bleeds
This path so deceptive
Reaching for better means
Something not so aggressive

I deal with
What's been dealt
Through the blood that's just stained
How can I forget my old self

It's my conviction
It's all that I deserve
Like a prowler in the shadows
Not living nor heard

Abandoned by myself
Best not to understand
For living in this hell
Creates forsaken sin

Wishing this was all a bad dream
My eyes open wide
Roaming aimlessly
It's so dark I can't find
The way through my own head

I suffer
I grieve
I wish upon death

Like it always had meaning

I walk this dark path
I've never felt so alone
It's better that I suffer
I'll find my way home

Feeling Free

I feel like world's shining down on me
This day is so unique
There's nothing that stands between

I'm full of love and its growth
Symbolized within my actions
At a time when I need it most

Inviting with open arms
It has been far too long
Since I've satisfied the things I've lost

Trust in these stable hands
With all I understand
Finding hope when it appears

Holding true to my form
There's so much I've displaced
Or poured out wrong

For the days I feel there's no assault
My head's clear of all the pain
I'm starting to feel results

Shacking loose this wobbly prop
Standing free on my own
My vices are at a loss

It feels good to awake
Trusting in the day
The sun rises with fulfillness
Instead of the typical aura of dismay

I'm dignified
It's what I see with these eyes
As free as my will
I stand with all my might
Capturing the moment
Absorb all its worth
I believe in this life before me
Now my soul sets its course

Into the Darkness

Free me from your prison of misery and hate
These illusions I can't defeat
Playing slave to its game

This petulant thesis is my curse
Peering verse to verse
It's so relevant and diverse

Seems the anguished
Deciphered my oppression
To reconcile the demented
That were trapped
By their indiscretions

Their intrusions I can't escape
Helpless to this fate
Chanting scripts to detain

I'm their victim
Imprisoned in shadow form
Following the sense of nothing
Into your world
I'm just born

Idolize upon the ground you stand
Lurking from the darkness
Only in light
I'm your friend

Mimicking your motions
Predicting your every move
This life is torture
Not sure
If I'll pull through

The light accentuates
I'm forced like a slave
Within a world of pretend
Deliver me back to my grave

Burning here for days
Thoughts been on pause
Relapsed his own endeavors
You'll find your faults

I'm the shadow of your world
The essence of your life
Walk me to the darkness
Let me consume what is mine

Make Me Whole

What drives me to deceive
This voice never rests
Self-imposed
Like some fiend
Derived from thoughts suppressed

I've tried to heal
To be all about love
Yet the inner me has this shield
Denying a sense I've lost

Every time I fight
It loses its appeal
I'm like this dark sickened blight
Who exposes a false deal

I've tried to free myself
Just a moment to break away
How do I redeem my health
When mentally
I'm not sane

Foolishly infused
JUST MAKE IT ALL STOP
I stand as living proof
Life's what I've lost

Testing my patience
Collectively just sick
Passively debating
Before my heart quits

Falling to find
Crushing my own pride
Slaughtered my dignity
You're not a spokesman of this mind
Needing to unwind
To gain some control
There's only so much I can take
Life in small dose

With hope I'm not feeling
This sense isn't free
Tricking my patience
To hang hope
As you'll see

Fear sets in motion
Do I run or just prepare
My conscience goes unspoken;
A look like he don't care

You did this
A voice murmurs from inside
All these elements help you fight
If there's no love
You won't survive

Suffocating

Suffocating
Every situation baring down
Contemplating my options
Times unbound

Settling in to embrace what's at stake
Giving in to this mayhem
Means I've lost the game
The revocation
Too confusing to relate
How could life dictate
These times I debate

My end draws near

Gasping for my last breath
As the air thickens
Filling with regret

My eyes tear

Hopeless to refute
I guess on this day
I won't live up to all I knew

Dazed
Too dizzy to regain
In my head is all this shame
With no time to retrace

Footsteps that lead so wrong
This path of sorrow
My strength just gone

Dropping to my knees
My resilience growing weak
Reaching one last time
Someone hear my plea

Without You

The day begins
Darkness still fills the skies
As I reminisce toward things
I've lived and let die

It's my life
To understand who I am
Analyze to withstand
Hope and I not hand and hand

You'd never triumph
It's sense I could never implore
I know what you're thinking
Settle me in
Feel the norm

Try to tame this conscience
Condone to live and praise
I'm just hooked on this demon
Chained like its slave

Fastened so tight
You couldn't tell us apart
To live by our own consensus
How we feel we are

Sickens me
How you think you can remain
Remember
We've tried it your way
Now I'm fragile
Some think just crazed

This dark desolate world gives me life
Alone
I find strength
Without you by my side

These eyes open
With sense you couldn't give
Devoted to this concept
It's my life
Here I live

Binding Souls

Nothing so unique
As what our hearts feel
Tempered by so many emotions
Strongly revealed
To embellish its existence
I can't emphasize enough
As beautiful as you are
One look makes my heart stop
The soothing comfort of a touch
As I'm closing my eyes
Thoughts you left to imagine
Never rest inside
Utterly crippled
Bound by you
This form of emotion
Binding truth
You're like my forbidden treasure
I cherish like gold
Your life I'd treat no different
Binding souls
To feel your heart thump
So steadily against mine
As the warmth of our feelings surrender
Love is blind
Inviting temptation
With every moment spent
We build something special through our own consensus

Lay It to Rest

Inside my head
Screaming to be free
This struggle of an endless note
Captivating my sanity

A fading tune
Fallen fears
Into this basin I've wept
For so many years

Playing a tune
For I'm intrigued
It's time to lay it to rest
Putting this mind at ease

To finally retain what I've ensured
Ending all this madness
Yet timid of course

Silent and still
Holding my breath
One little movement
I'd be scared to death

Inside my head
The rhythm turns bleak
Echoes through this hollow
Place I felt free

Lost in motion
Still as a corpse
It's so relentless
This fear I encourage

I want it to end
Yet it seems
Every time I forget
It seeks to imprison me grieving

I can't take it
These headaches this pain
They keep giving me stuff
To help me stay sane

Freaked of the world
Freaking on myself
Involuntary form of emotion
I'm just letting it out

Locked Away

Try to find peace
Maybe a little serenity
This hardship of grief
Overtakes my integrity

Intentions institutionalized
Locked away without a key
I've pieced together the acts that make life
So clear they could teach

I'm not crazed
Nor thought to be insane
Living by your formality
I don't belong in this place

Another victim
Toward your beliefs
Lashing out
Being violent
While you sedate every tendency

I've sorted it through
Time and time again
You think me a fool
With these acts of defiance

Constantly deceived
Locking me away
Like a freak without a dream
Your conducts just fake

I'll forgive all your schemes
Forget these theatrics
My head can't be breached

I hear nothing
The whole world becomes a blur
Fading away
To a place that's safe
Or at least
I hope
Really not sure

Could I Be

Every day is the same
This repetitive sea of emotions
Drowning in its wake
I'm back on track
With all that I hate
It all seems predictable
This tide pointless to escape

I must confess
Seems I'm possessed by the haunting
Everything I try to process
Entities become so taunting

Is this really me
A reflection without a face
Trying to decipher these conflicts
Between the living and pretend

I exist because of you
What else could explain
These intervals aren't a fluke?

Here and there
By or gone
You're always in my head
Your mayhem clinching strong

Just give me a day
Set my thoughts free
Let's form a unity
Live as life seems

Normal in our own state of mind
Banish your world to be forgotten
You're not a friend of mine

Come to terms with all that I'm thinking
Wish I could flip a switch
So peace could fill this prison

Drifting away
By the waves of sorrow
Enable me to cleanse my soul today
I'll let myself worry about tomorrow

Never Again

Just never my soul again
Sometimes I find these walls
Absorbed into a life of sin
Seeing these sights
I can't run nor hide
I'm a victim in life
In scenes I can't fight
Where will my soul send
Acting out the moments
Like it was all pretend
Just never my soul again

I perish this dark lie
Because the truth had no flight
A voice too small to understand

You let my soul beg
Through eyes
I cry
Reborn this soul I dread
Where shall my soul send
I wish to awake
Without being trapped in your stay
Making me touch and play once again
Just never my soul again
Through the darkness I find
Though years pass
I'm not right
This imperial life begins

My eyes tear
Alone in deep thoughts
Where shall my soul send
Inflicting cuts I can't stop
Through bloodshed
They might pronounce me dead
Where shall my soul send
As the darkness takes toll
Invited to a world
Feeling hope is dead
I cut up my pride to assure this time
It wasn't a game of pretend
What you've taken isn't right
As I bleed here each night
Like the past only seeks revenge
Why can't this soul forget
To live and be free without entrapment of grief
These voices say my soul is dead

My Flame

In the depths of the world
Deceived
Still bleeding
Trying to retrieve doubt
To find a meaning

Is it the way of these so cold days
Burning
Yet my soul's blazed
Still fueling my heart's pain

Walking into a fire that one starts
While you relate
Anticipating that desire
Internally your thoughts cross

A soul stray
With a feeling it's never obtained
My mind elevates with fear
As you just lie to feel safe

I'm hanging on to every night
What I once thought was so special
Fades in due time

So in-depth I do plead
Surrendering its meaning
For my life does see
Every action that betrays
You think I'm blind
When it comes to those points
I retract
Why fuel a fire
Only to embrace cold nights?

To believe my world was saddened
Only I control
For my passion is pride
My flame only exceeds to such heights
For you
Its dim died

I Can't Escape

Something's telling me I'm going to die
Voices so strange
I'm questioning truth to life
So obscure
As I try to link together my own doubt
This place I thought pure
I'm not even safe from myself
Fueled by my own dire need
I subsequently imagine
To feel free with peace
Echoes of tone that I can never make out
Murmurs through the darkness
Of this forbidden Hell
The feeling of peace slips away
Closing my eyes to embrace
The solitude I create
My retentions mean nothing more
Then the fact I give in
To this sorrow-stricken world
What am I thinking?
Does this stem from my regret?
My conscience has me debating
When I take my last breath

FEAR

Sometimes the fear's so haunting
Feeling crippled toward its need
To overcome these things so often
Leaving me here to plead

In the depths of its desire
Conflicts I can't evade
There's so much that transpires
I balance it all with a different face

Imaging the charisma to overcome
The threat of a darker meaning
Enlighten this world so strung
My intuition passively revealing

The bells of death
Leading me to silence
Into the darkness I forget
There's no sense of reliance

Bleeding thoughts
That mentally can't compute
This restless soul
So in depth
Nothing could refute

A little too late to stop
Captivating my lonely world
Enough is enough
Standing at the gate of the absurd

Who holds the key
This demented man seeks
Repress that feeling of death
I furiously so need

Can't control these emotions
In my head
Bound to its commotion
Self-torture became my friend
I scream
For as long as my thoughts still breathe
If it all comes baring down
My pride you can't defeat

THE STRUGGLE

Throughout it all
I've always maintained
A sensible life
For I had to find strength

Nothing was given
I struggled every day
With a screwed-up head
A broken home
A childhood full of shame

Addiction was my comfort
For every moment I can forget
I grew up fast as the years just pass
That comfort was just a test

What I needed was closure
To find out who I was
Facing the demon
That left my head feeling
That this world had no love

My minds stained
Seeing your face every day
Raping me of my purity
As a child I couldn't say
NO!
Now here I'm bleeding
NO!
My innocence deceived when
Your thoughts were so wrong

Living so confused
I owe this to you
Took all I had
To realize the truth

Living with these impressions
Raped and abused
Objected to your obsessions
My life is living proof

No matter what happens
You can be strong
Take what's inside
Bring your thoughts to light
Stand for who you are

Figurative State

A sense with no control
Clinically insane
We'll show
They oppose
Selflessness remains

It's a figurative state
You can't gauge
What you won't face
Regressions elected
Yet the world can't relate

These objectives
Inviting themes
It's beyond your comprehension
Pointless to conceive
Like illusions of normality
People try to seize
This balance so obscene
Figments of your
Fractured dreams
Slowly deplete
Obscuring the delusion
The rest remain mundane
Never to receive themes of fame
Real life's interface
Integrates but a taste
Of what
It can't explain

Sufferance schemes
Concepts you couldn't fathom
Intercepting these points to plead
Guiding the demented
We're all quite intrigued

LIFE

To place a thought
Ponder upon its meaning
It's like a gift that can't be taught
Comprehending
My words
These feelings

I express what's all so unique
So deep and out of reach
Most wouldn't believe

So fortunate to be granted
Some days it's my curse
Misfortune leads to dwelling
Which brings me back to this source

This fear that can never escape
While I'm here
Exploiting all I am

This is it
I've chartered my course
If this is the path I must follow
I'll contribute to its worth

Anticipating
The thoughts only I would know
Laying them all out
Can you grasp the concepts I unfold

Thinking deep
Letting my words flow through your mind
Twisting my own fate
Time after time

Become as one
As you sift through all you hear
Your lack of sense and comprehension
Steers you clear

I'm so much more
Than words jotted down
I'm a live link to a mind
Truly divine

Losing Focus

No matter what I do
Or say
This inner torment
Completely deranged

It's hard to maintain
When all seems collective
The root of my evil
Reflects its deception

I grasp for things that aren't there
It's my reality that's confused
These delusions make me impaired

Frequently timid
There's so much to embrace
Feeling my reality slipping
Into a world I can't maintain

Maybe this is that journey
To end my own grief
Somewhere in this world
There must be a key

To free me from this torment
Reflecting my sane self
Free me from what lies dormant
My conscience is my hell

I feel its heavy hand with each path I walk
Is it good
Or is it bad?
Depending on which one of me you cross

Just Let Me Be

Some people think I'm a little crazed
Because of the ways I freely feel
Turn a page
Jot it down
Emotions tend to build
Let me be
My life feels better
When I'm not a caged-up little freak

There's so much to overcome
Why take it on alone
When all I need is my pad and pen
My thoughts tend to flow

That's just me
Head strong
As my emotions freely bleed

I can't take all the pressure
Bottled inside
Turing toward the things
That seem normal to my
Everyday life
Just let me be

I'm just a victim of what I can't hide
My life is an open book
So free in mind
This freedom of expression
Just defines
The way I interpret
Is my given right
It's just me

Through the Ashes

Terror arises from the ash of my sins
Charred remains sum
This fortune I can't win
This feeling reduced
Taking so quickly to the breeze
All that remained
Was an imprint of someone I couldn't be

If this is all too bearing
My way of life seems so scary
I never figured you would come this far
Nothing's ordinary
When you're clinched to a demon
Its abrasive methods resemble a god

I walk among this world
To feel no pain
Nothing could ever faze this person I create
I truly set myself free
All it took was to lose it all
To discover a better being

Internally
I'll never feel the same
Peeled away
Layers of my soul's grace

To attune what I've sustained
I suffer
I've lost
Burned to the point I can't cross
Even if heaven had a gate

Sifting through the ash of my sins
I'd sacrifice it all
Before this demon could infringe

Consume Me

Fueled by the things I can't help
In the darkness
I find dreams
All I thought were lost
This time I've crossed
A point I've never seen
Disrupted by the images
Questioning my reality

Take a look
I mean deep into my eyes
Follow the footsteps
This path well defined

Embrace the fear that assaults
Whisper into the darkness
Through this forsaken hell

I'm still shaking so shattered
Feeling there's no other way
Condemned to torment
Because it understands my heart's pain

Souls and fiends consume this world
Swallowing the anguished
It's all they know

Years pass
My dreams remain
Haunted by the memories
I can't replace
Like a disease spreading inside
I cure it with every supplement not legal in life

The bottles
My friend
Down to every last drop
Is this what I must go through?
Just make these dreams stop

It's like I'm possessed
I've lost all control
Living with disruption
With nowhere to turn
I'm always trapped within my head
For days on end
Repeating the same path
Because I can't find a new beginning

Feelings shrivel
Only to be peeled away
It's all so absurd
How the pain remains

Stepping forth
With the intent to face my fear
It's as dark as my ambitions
For which I'm prepared
Don't let it consume me

Help Me Forget

Feeling this time
Like it's all in vain
Another day gone to waste
No two thoughts seem to change
If I can pull on through
This bitter place

Just let me forget
Help me escape
When all I have left
Is this fear I can't shake

Ripping and tearing
This emotional fringe
Shredding that peace
Sheltered from sins

Fulfilling my reasons
They'll slip away
Down to the place
Where I lay to rest my heart's pain

Help me believe
Help me forget
Needing to retrieve
More than regrets

Some days feel better
Others just seem
So full of hatred
Like the shadows of my dreams
Needing something to ease
I take a deep breath

This road I walk
Is the way I repress
It all seems senseless
Help me forget

WHAT to LIVE BY

With all the things we go through
Life is a test beyond our belief
Trials never seen
Nor could deem them complete

Following the path
Letting it lead me where it may
Open thoughts into this world I cross
For a sense without mistakes

To become my meaning
Defining purpose as it appears
Rendering to absolution
To better understand

These principles of substance
A fortune of unshown truth
What we display or all we create
Glory upon thy stoop

To stand so proud
With all you envision
Carry on with hope
To implement your decisions

Your soul should be unbound
Never to fall under misfortune
Each head wears its own crown
For all to be devoted

DIFFERENT FORMS

I've lost myself
In a world that provokes me
A misfit among convictions
My delirious fate is doomed
I'm not stable
Leading a life revolting
These feuds on relapse
Pertinacious acts are proof

How I'm wired isn't right
That I have no self-control
Who implements these decisions
This dire man unfolds

I'm just a timid soul
Looking for a place to hide
If I was rigid as cold steel
I'd structure a way of life

I can't grasp
Sentiments that form and teach
This reality is blind
Toward your vigorous passive pleas
Set me free as rain falls from skies
I'm sick of obsessing over theories I bring to light

Just a pawn
Fallen victim to conclusions
Drowning here in fear
This outcome not so soothing

Temptation always speaks of pain
No matter how you're disguised
Among this masquerade

Can't break through all these compulsions
Randomly thinking
Sets my thoughts in motion

Seclusion becomes my life
I rid myself of corruption
Sorting through false ties

This feels like a prison
Misery holds the key
If I devised a provision
I'd force that form to flee

I can't take it
Everything ends in vain
Feeling my soul erupting
Which part of me remains

Masks

What creates this thing I call life
The balance always shifting
Within its lies
I act so pure in heart
Yet my devious perception
Tears through my own thoughts

I swear upon my innocence
People perceive me all the same
What they don't see
This mask so prevalent
Over the darkness it pertains

To hide who I really am
People judge and put down
I'm suited nor prepared

Where do I turn
As I take it all in?
I'm an ill-minded delegate
With a delirious way of thinking

All I've assumed has shattered who I am
Left with a stitched-up illusion
People can't understand

I laugh
As I fade into my place of comfort
This solitude of corruption
Consumed by its justice

My former self I had to let go
Upon the sacrificial altar
Within this dark forsaken hell

You couldn't feel through the depths of these eyes

My views so passive
Walking through
The hollows of my mind
I'm just free

Reflecting What

When do my fears get washed away?
I can't forget the reality of my grief
In all these misplaced dreams
Every scar bares a symbol
Within that moment maybe crazed
Sometimes my own feelings are little out of place
What's wrong with my reality
Timid toward what you think
Judged by misconceptions
I'm as foul
As the days are bleak
Running low on options
I can't be subjected to this light
Seeking comfort in the shadows
Till the world turns night
I'm everything I'd never thought I'd be
In the face of my own dream
My world's sold to this theme
Unmasking its deception
I now realize what I've been
I can't pretend another day
It's who I was
Not what I am

Life Astray

Uncover my soul bursting in tears
Looking toward the world
Save me from this fear
Alone
Such a hollow place
I'm as shallow as the grave
They dug for my death
The thumping of my heart echoes through this keep
Alone in silence
Tears fall to its beat

This destiny has no pardon to explain
Don't think I'll regress
From living life astray
Mentally detained
Like these walls are closing in
So much for being safe
From my own self-inflictions

I scream in silence
Because it's in my head
This life has no balance
Left here for dead
These incisions keep seeping
Purities lost
Relentlessly inflicting
This reality won't stop
Twisted thoughts
Losing time
Segments pester
Fragile minds

Dreams unspoken
To define its lies
Fragments fractured
Fragile lives

Where does it end
I passively suppress
I can't stand among the living
Buried within regret

Can't recollect
A meaning without restraint
What I lack is
A sense of conquest
Or deliverance to embrace

This Is the End

Getting a grip on who I am
Searching for reasoning
In this world who's playing

Conflicted
With these series of events
Bound to these conflicts that circle my head
I think I'm just dead
Inside my mind
Infused with madness
I thrive to unwind
Needing to be free
Let me live life
I need to release
Times of unsettled vibes
Perpetrating the demon
That's still leading the fight

I can't live
By the justice of its grief
How can I maintain my own stature
Chained to its dream

Watching my world
Burn before my eyes
These visions that tears blind
Reality dies
For every longing moment
Within
I find the strength

For the end
I'm not knowing
Will I break or be tamed?

I'm falling fast
For these days I can't show
My life's on relapse
I can't break these chains of old
This demon takes control
Fusing its pain
It's the deepest of devotions
Feelings that can't change
I give and just take
Closing my eyes
Within I shatter
Another day in my life

The end draws near
Along with that last bit of hope
Shedding my last tear
Fading into a shadow unknown

Wash Away My Fear

So unsettled
Every feeling surrounding my mind
These days I'm so unstable
No reasoning to my life

I break through
To live with these assaults
Given the circumstances
What I fear is the end result

Captivate my sanity
At the whims of destruction
This time I can't evade
Shedding tears
To wash away my fear
A burden I purge
Because I know there's no escape

All that I believe
Every word that's spoken loud
If I could bring my thoughts to reality
My fear would have no grounds

A chance to be free
Grasping my integrity
To utilize its means

I want to live without corruption
Vanquish these tears
To live without disruption
Till this fear disappear

CONSCIENCE

I've never stopped running
Seems I'm breaking down
I can't overcome the aliment sorta bound
It's always in me
Day after day
This ridiculous fucking voice   in my head
Used to speak so gingerly
Keeping me safe
Certainly has delivered
A derivative state
But years of waste
Has taken its toll
Haunted by its fury
Life unfolds
I made you   can't you see
Murmurs intently
In spite of pleas
Falling fast
Losing control
Wrapped around a concept
With nowhere to turn
A haunting laugh
Echoes through the silence of the night
Followed by a whisper that chilled my whole life
You can never escape me

One Step Closer

When do I feel sane?
This solitude has been corrupted
Through living lies astray
A firm grip
They walk me with no shame
To a place among the forgotten
All that exists is pain
Hopes shattered dreams
Memories start to fade
The clanking of these chains
Reminds me it's all too late

I'm led to this fractured stone
Stained by the innocence
All to capture their souls

Their blood dripping
My conscience fades
Drastically thinking
Maybe it's a mistake

If I could supersede your ambitions
Relinquish to explain
I hold no place among the sinnest
My soul's more than just a slave

Upon the stone
I'm asked to speak my last words
Lifting my head
I'm so distraught
My purpose finally shown

Free this mind
My life is yours to take
My soul is bound by blood;
For you
It will never obey

Something to Embrace

Empty words
Violent minds
Physically compliant
Toward thoughts defined

Embrace what
Only few know
This start to a new beginning
True to our growth

Giving into this world
With so many dreams
Even through the fog
That seems to infringe

Through all the evil that conforms
Determining my fate
You look at me and smile
Like you're not even fazed

With you I'm never guessing;
You're as pure as they come
Filling my heart
Even when I said I can't love
The warmth of your comfort
Feeling every smile your soul brings
Brightens my day
In ways not seen

To you my spirit
Your undying endeavors
Free me from this world
I shall never question

For too long

I've wondered with nothing to embrace
You're like my gift from the heavens
Through your essence
I find strength

To become what I've lost
In so many dreams
You're that feeling I just love;
You give me something to embrace

THE DARKEST DAY

I've crossed so many different paths
Some defined
While others designed
To hold my whole life back

I'm a prospect of what most can't concede
With emotions strung so deep
My own demon set me free

I've crashed through the abyss
A place so depraved
My own shadow said
"Fuck this!"

To endure what most can't compute
I tantalize these old wounds
To understand the truth

Laying my whole life to waste
As you lead me to this place
In spite of all the pain

To cast aside one's pride
For days lock inside
Their reasons cannot die

Their intent crawling up my skin
Attacking my conscience
Leaving me hollow as my sins

I keep dragging these old chains
To wander in this place
No purpose
No strength to escape

Dreams That Might

If each night could just last
This fear you revoke would collapse
Feeling a sense that you're free
Needing to unwind
Clinched to a mentality that defines
Hopes and peace within arm's reach

Fading to a place
Beauty reflecting your soul
Imagining the tranquility
Fading into dreams unknown

Another step closer
Seems too late
How could something so taunting
Now be withered and plagued?
Appears before you
Lands that die
This is how you interpret
Your dreams of life

Connecting the pieces
All in dismay
They'd show a better way of living
If you conform to its fate

Looking beyond
As you set your mind free
Everything reveals
Truth and meaning

Walking you through
A place where thoughts come alive
Thankful it's a dream
Not my real life

Into the Shadows

I step into the shadows
Every day
The light's just fading
Not sure if I can handle
Showing my face today
Feeling so elusive
I believe there are no conclusions
Can someone please show me
How to live again?

Torn from the balance
Shifting grief over powers
Vile is this world
Through shattered eyes I see
Its control goes unnoticed
Absorbing what's left of purpose
Controlling who I am

Choosing to conform this way
Dimmed are the lights
Like existence always fades
Never to apprehended that demon
I'm too numb to tame

To believe things could flourish
While I suffocate
Bruised and tarnish
A better place to be
Just locked away
To dreary lies that breed

Picturing life still posing
Beauty and all it's showing
I visualize from the shadows
I'm not as vigorous as my world of dreams

Every day the light's just fading
Not sure how to handle
Everything I was shown this day
Fades into shadows unseen

Stranger

I hold it in
This pain that I feel
Consumed with sin
I know won't heal

To awake with such shame
This reflection asks why
Through the depths you'll retain
As reasoning collides

It's hard to refute
When you felt it firsthand
Confusion well induced
Years passed that weren't sane
It's like I'm on trial for all that's mistaken
I'm the victim of my past
No sense of erasing

Consumed by this hatred you promote
Without a just cause
Enabled the intricacy of its growth
Abused
By your selfish need to amuse
Raping my innocence
These secrets bare truth

This isn't a fable of my life
As you proceed to entice me
Night after night

As a youth I couldn't explain
It seems so normal
Every night before bed

Sleeping with a stranger
Not knowing what's right
Turning it into a game
So I'd suck him all the time

Sheltering its meaning
Close like we were friends
To the point I enjoyed our dark moments
And wanted it before bed

What were you thinking
This stranger I don't know
As years passed
I've imprisoned these feelings of doubt

Ripping and tearing
At the purity of my thoughts
Images of our moments
Never seize to stop

I fight here to explain
Like I fight every day to erase
It's something I must live with
This stranger in my bed

Dead I'm Just Gone

WAIT!
There's something controlling my mind
STAINED!
The memories left there left there to die
Deserted
I don't deserve this
What could quench or sa   tis   fy

Conflicting lies
Fearing your own despair
It's so revealing
Yet your pride's not willing to share

Punishing to prove
The pain's by far
The best truth
As you tear through your own flesh

Deserving
These voices I'm serving
Enticed by the torment they inflict
WAIT!
There's something controlling my mind
STAINED!
By the memories
Damn they can't hide
I don't deserve this
All these feeling just surface
Prisoned by circumstance
Left here to die

Conform to its demand
Too weak to dismiss
Cutting my life to waste
Only hope
Can visualize my distress

Where does the pain go from here?
No matter how much I bleed
Still lonely in tears

I could drain the last drop
Of my own beating heart
It's as stubborn as my thoughts;
Damn
It won't stop!
Sought out for repentance
So desperate to retrieve
I'll admit that I'm demented
For a life with no grief
WAIT!
These voices screaming
I'm stepping back to where I belong
STAINED!
By my blood
Scribed on this tombstone
Dead I'm just gone

Awake Me

Schemes of unwanted dreams
Depriving my peace
Memories go unseen
I'm trying to deplete
Overthrowing my integrity
This personal being

To absorb so kindly
Nothing can escape
This course that I'm finding
Tearing through hell's gate

Shivering through my soul
Nothing's at ease
I know it all too well
Feelings strung so deep
Breaking through this sanction
Passing through what seems
The halls of torment
Souls filled with grief

Another assault
My eyes fear the darkness of this place
Grasping my head with force
Gasping for a breath to take

Timid as fear intertwines
This interface keeps revealing
Images you can't fight

Determined to deceive
Inside the demon forms
There was a time I felt so free
Now I'm not so sure

Imbued to this soul of death
I can feel as it devours
Panicking and shaking
My purity it overpowers

Screaming here in vain
I know my end is near
Someone awake me please!
Make these dreams disappear

Who Hears Me

A sequence of unrelated events
Sculpted into a masterpiece
Fragments of my own perception

Concluded years from birth
Conclusions resulting in a not-so-literal art

Massive schemes
Discovered lies
As you picture existence
Such repulsive times

Thoughts of a screwed-up mind
With only shame it retains
Never fades nor strays
For days I place

Uncertainly covers me blind
To stand determined
I'm so persistent
At just living life

Frivolous yet refined
Devious with a price to pay with pride
A con of lie
I conjure whatever can spare me
To face my own light

Flushed away with rivers and tides
Eroding my own sense
For that I strive

This endless fight
Grips my own fear
Could never make things right
I shed a lone tear

Screaming through the darkness
Who hears my thoughts?
My echo fades through the hollows
Every moment feels lost

Inner Me

I came here to let my heart bleed
Not knowing what to do
For my world to please

Lost my emotions
Like I'm impaired
Nothing ever soothes
The pleasure's not fair

Engaged in acts that aren't me
It's a parade of lustful feelings
I'm looking to reprieve

There's a piece of someone I know is still alive
Lingering in the shadows
Its place of life

Banished my former self
If I could find a way to grasp
Before this reality rebels

Searching for this timid soul
Hiding from its captures
In this hellish world

Baring down
Such infusive ties
If I look to be distraught
Such confusing times

These days I feel without a soul
Something is always missing
The balance between my worlds

Breaking the seal of trust
Because I can't comprehend

Alone

Lost in thoughts
Back to where it began

I search
Like there's no tomorrow
Crossing through such wretched places
Even the devil wouldn't follow

All to find my essence
To know still exists
For now
I'll let it be
But my search will still persist

Sea of Sins

There's so much you don't see
I'm living
No cares
No prison
Upon my own intuition
Intoxicate this sea for sinning

No one understands these times
Letting my world crumble before my eyes
Gripping firmly
Because I can't let go
My life's slipping on this downward slope

Can't you see I'm living
No cares
No prison
Feeling dreams fall from skies
Faster and faster
As you drown in life

Intoxicated by this sea of sins
Constellation of my fear bottled within
There's so much you can't see
I'm feeling
This is my escape
From life's dealings

Constant conflicts
Turmoil provoked
I refuse to believe
I'm at the end of my rope
Constructive interests
More so in dose
It's condescending
This life I chose

This world
My prison
I drift alone to embrace
My sea of sins
Sum up my shame

This world's devious
So full of delight
Step into its shadow
An urge you can't fight

Suppress all that's revealed
You're at the last of your substance
For the day that appealed

Another tear drops upon the sea
Blacked out with no shame
Losing your integrity

As your body collapses
You know can't win
You'll wake up in the morning
Back to your sea of sins

CPSIA information can be obtained
at www.ICGtesting.com
Printed in the USA
LVOW11*1449250318
571080LV00006B/40/P